Dedicated to : J.T. , M.J. , Harmony
Parents, Students, Teachers

SUPERFRIENDS
Against
BULLYING

Well this story starts on September 3rd, on a warm and sunny morning, it's the first day of school in Critterville. This day is also a special day for everyone in the community of Critterville, as it is the first day for all the businesses to be open for business. Slowly one by one the candle lights from all the homes, in Critterville came on as the folks in Critterville were waking up from their beds, to get ready for their big day. Everyone was nervous, but none as nervous as Bandit Raccoon. Mrs. Raccoon went down to the kitchen, and started breakfast, while Mr. Raccoon went to wake Bandit and Bonnie, and told them to get ready for school.

After Bonnie and Bandit were up, and getting ready for their first day of school, Mr. Raccoon joined Mrs. Raccoon in the kitchen, and waited for breakfast. The smell of blueberry pancakes, and syrup filled the kitchen. Bonnie was dressed, and down in the kitchen in no time, and ready to eat. Bandit on the other hand wasn't in no hurry, because he was very nervous, about the first day of school. By the time Bandit went down to the kitchen to eat, Mr. Raccoon was already in his furniture shop making furniture for the orders he had gotten. Bonnie was out helping Mr. Edison the owl delivering the Critterville newspapers, which Bandit was suppose to be helping with.

Bandit sat quietly down at the table, as Mrs. Raccoon gave him a plate of blueberry pancakes, smothered in maple syrup. Then Bandit spoke, in a low voice, saying, "Good morning mom, and thank you for the pancakes and the juice." Mrs. Raccoon being the mother she is; sensed Bandit had something upsetting him. Mrs. Raccoon stopped what she was doing, and sat down in the chair beside Bandit to see what was bothering him. Mrs. Raccoon put her arm around her son Bandit, and asked, "What is upsetting you Bandit?"

Bandit quietly said, "There's nothing wrong mom." Then Mrs. Raccoon looked at Bandit over top of her glasses, with a serious look of concern. She said, "Now Bandit you can fool a lot of folks; but you can't fool your mom, I know you too well. Your father does the same thing. When he has something upsetting him, he'll keep it to himself instead of asking for help or talking about it, but here lately your father talks about things upsetting him, and he said just by talking to someone about it makes him feel a lot better." Then Mrs. Raccoon told Bandit to get what was upsetting him, off his mind and talk to her. Then she said,

"Maybe I could do or say something to help you, with whatever is up setting you."

Then Bandit slowly looked up at his mom and said, "I'm scared to go to school." Then Mrs. Raccoon asked Bandit, "What scares you about going to school son?" Bandit thought about his mom's question and responded, "I'm scared of what the other kids, and Mr. Edison would think of me, if I did something wrong." Mrs. Raccoon replied, "Bandit dear, as long as you do your best, that's all anyone can ask from you, and that's all you can ask from yourself." Then Mrs. Raccoon said, "No one expects you to know everything. Us grown-ups don't know everything either. There's an old saying, that everyone learns something every day, and I for one will agree with that old saying. Now if you make a mistake, or give a wrong answer to a question, that's how we all learn Bandit, we learn from our mistakes. So don't feel bad when you make a mistake, because everyone makes mistakes, and learns from them. Now Bandit has anything I've said made you feel better?" Bandit put on a happy face, and said, "Thank you very much mom." But deep down, Bandit was still very nervous about the day in front of him at school. Bandit was so nervous, he couldn't finish his breakfast. Then Bandit grabbed his book bag, and told his mom he was going to see his dad at the Furniture Shop before school.

Once there, Bandit talked with his father Mr. Raccoon about an order of chairs for Mrs. Snow a swan who owned the Critterville Boarding house which his father was working on. Just then Mr. Raccoon asked if he would help paint the chairs after school. Bandit replied, "Yes I was hoping I could help you." Then Mrs. Raccoon came in the door of the shop, and gave Bandit his lunch. Bandit said, "Thank you mom," as the Critterville school teacher Mr. Edison rang the bell to let the children know, the first day of school was about to begin.

As Bandit went out the door of his father's shop, his parents wished him good luck on his first day. Mrs. Raccoon watched out the window of the shop, as Bandit slowly made his way to school. Mr. Raccoon saw the worried looked on his wife's face, and told her, "Do not worry, Bandit will be all right. Besides Mr. Edison is a good teacher and

I'm sure he will help Bandit get through the first day." Mrs. Raccoon smiled, as she watched Bandit, Mr. Edison and the rest of the children disappear into the school.

Meanwhile, in the school, all the children was sitting quietly at their desks. Mr. Edison stood in front of the classroom, as he showed the children the blackboard, using a pointer to go over the activities, he planned for the first day of school. The first activity Mr. Edison had planned, is for the children to stand up at their desks, and tell everyone their name, a little bit about themselves, and their favorite hobbies. With this activity the children would be to get to know each other better. Mr. Edison began the activity, first by telling the children his name and that his favorite hobbies were reading books and fishing.

Then one by one, the children of Critterville stood up at their desks each saying, their names and their favorite hobbies with Bandit being the last one. Mr. Edison sensed that Bandit was really nervous and a bit scared from the tremble in his voice, as he told everyone his name and his favorite hobbies were fishing and making furniture with his dad. Then Bandit quickly sat back down at his desk, accidentally knocking his book bag, and his lunch off his desk and onto the floor.

The children surprised Bandit when they didn't laugh or make fun of him for accidentally knocking things to the floor. All the children except the two hedgehogs, Porky and Corky, who both laughed quietly whispered at Bandit calling him names such as, clumsy, and other names. As Mr. Edison turned to the blackboard with his pointer to read the second activity, he had planned for the day, Porky quickly got up from his desk, went over to Bandit picked up his lunch from the floor opened it, and took out a piece of pie that Bandit had in his bag for lunch. Then he left Bandit's lunch bag open and then dumped the rest of his lunch on the floor, while calling Bandit clumsy. Porky then went back to his desk, while on his way back he flicked some of the other children's ears as he passed by.

This caused a few of the other children Foxy, Hazel, Bazel, and Clay to yell ouch, as they grabbed their ears. Porky quietly sat down at his desk, before Mr. Edison turned around to see what was wrong. Mr. Edison turned to see what has happened, and he saw that Bandit was upset and that Hazel, Bazel, Foxy, and Clay also looked upset as they held their ears. Mr. Edison asked the children what was wrong with a concerned tone in voice. The children saw Porky and Corky clinching their fists, while looking at them with a mean look. Bandit and the other children were scared of them due to being bullied, so they simply answered saying that nothing was wrong. Then Mr. Edison, once again turned back to the blackboard, to read the second activity he had planned.

Again Porky and Corky looked at Bandit, and the other children while quietly laughing at them, this made Bandit and the other children feel more upset and scared. Then Mr. Edison using his pointer, read the second activity, which was to give all the children notebooks, paper, pencils, and any supplies they would need. Mr. Edison told the children that all the school supplies, that they were getting was generously donated by Ranger Woods, and that their first assignment would be to send a thank you letter to Ranger Woods. Mr. Edison went over to the table, and opened the box full of school supplies that were all put together and ready for the children. At the top of each notebook had a name on for every student, so Mr. Edison then called each student over to the table to get their supplies.

He then went over to the blackboard to read the third activity. As Mr. Edison started to read the activity, he had seen Bandit raise his hand. Mr. Edison turned and asked, "Do you have a question Bandit?" Bandit replied, "Yes! Mr. Edison, where is my notebook and school supplies?" Mr. Edison looked surprised, and went back over to the boxes and saw that they were empty. Mr. Edison then looked over at Bandit, who had a small tear in his eye, and said, "I'm sorry Bandit, I'll ask Ranger Woods tonight to bring you some supplies tomorrow." Bandit replied, "Okay," trying to hide being upset, but Mr. Edison felt bad for young Bandit.

Once again, the two bullying hedgehogs Corky and Porky, saw that Bandit was upset and had tears swelling up in his eyes, they began quietly laughing and making fun of poor Bandit. They did it quietly so Mr. Edison could not hear them but made sure Bandit could hear them, as they made fun of him for being upset. They were calling him names, and balled their hands up and rubbed them under their eyes, as they made fun of him. Bandit saw the two bullying hedgehogs making fun of him. This made poor Bandit even more upset as a few more tears, that swelled up in his sad eyes, fell out onto his cheeks, and rolled down his face, causing the two bullies to make fun of him more.

As for the rest of the children in the classroom, they all felt sad for Bandit, as Bandit was their friend, and as they saw the two hedgehog brothers making fun of poor Bandit. They all began to become angry, and disliking the bullying brothers for what they were doing to Bandit. The two bullying brothers didn't care, as they continued to make fun of Bandit. They even looked at the other children and gave them mean looks. Mr. Edison looked over at young Bandit, and saw that he was very upset, not knowing that Porky and Corky were making fun of Bandit. Mr. Edison thought to himself, maybe I can cheer Bandit up, by having him help pass out the schoolbooks, which was the third activity that he had written on the blackboard.

Then Mr. Edison asked for four volunteers, to help pass out the schoolbooks. All the children raised their hands except for Bandit. Mr.

Edison picked Candy, who is a bear and Clay's sister, to help pass out the math books. He picked Porky to pass out the writing books, Foxy to pass out the spelling books, and he asked Bandit to pass out the science books. Bandit was doing fine, as he was passing out the science books until the two bullying hedgehog brothers Porky and Corky began to bully him again. This time while Bandit was passing out the science books, Porky who was passing out the writing books saw that his brother Corky stuck his foot out waiting to trip Bandit as he passed his desk with a stack of science books in his hands. Porky seeing what his brother was trying to do to Bandit, with a mean grin on his face, went up behind Bandit and pushed him to trip and drop the science books all over the floor.

When Bandit fell onto the floor, he landed on Skippy's tail, who is a squirrel. Skippy yelled and jumped up from his desk from the pain of Bandit falling onto his tail. Skippy jumped up so quickly that he then fell into Clay and Hazel, who were sitting in the desks in front of him, causing Clay, Hazel and himself to all fall to the floor. Seeing Skippy, Clay, Hazel and poor Bandit fall to the floor, Mr. Edison ran over to make sure they were all alright and to help them up. The two bullying hedgehog brothers Porky and Corky just stood back so that Mr. Edison wouldn't hear them, quietly laughing at poor Bandit and the mess that they caused by tripping Bandit. Bandit got up from the floor with tears of sadness in his eyes and rolling down his cheeks and said sorry to Skippy for falling onto his tail. Skippy replied, "Don't worry about it Bandit, it didn't hurt that bad. I know you didn't mean to do it." Then Bandit said sorry to Clay and Hazel for knocking them to the floor. Clay and Hazel looked at their sad friend Bandit and said, "It's okay Bandit." Clay and Hazel along with the other classmates began helping Bandit pick up the science books, all except for Porky and Corky, who were still quietly laughing at the mess and the pain they have caused to the others.

Mr. Edison saw the tears of sadness rolling down Bandit's cheeks and asked, "Are you okay, Bandit?" With tears still rolling down his cheeks as he looked over at the two hedgehog brothers, who were still quietly laughing and making fun of Bandit and answered, "Yes, Mr. Edison I am okay." Bandit's friends and classmates became angry as they saw the tears of pain and sadness roll down his face and seeing the two hedgehog brothers Porky and Corky were still laughing and making fun of their friend and making the rest of the students angry at the two hedgehog bullies. Clay who is Bandit's best friend, who didn't like to see his friend so upset knowing Bandit was having a bad day and knowing that Porky and Corky were making Bandit's day much worse by making fun of him and just being bullies, looked at Porky and Corky and said, "You two need to quit bullying Bandit and the others," with an angry look on his face. As Clay finished telling Porky and Corky to stop bullying Bandit, the rest of the children with angry faces began to say the same thing to Porky and Corky. Mr. Edison who was unaware of

Porky and Corky bullying Bandit and some of the other students in the class, had all the children calm down and sit down at their desks.

Then Mr. Edison with a worried and surprised look on his face asked Clay to please tell him what Porky and Corky were doing to Bandit and some of the other students. Clay stood up from his desk and told Mr. Edison about how Porky and Corky were making fun of Bandit and some of the other students. Clay told Mr. Edison that when Bandit tripped passing out the science books, Porky and Corky made him trip on purpose causing him to fall to the floor, with the science books in his hands. Then Clay went on to say that what Porky and Corky were doing to Bandit and the other students was wrong and mean and he decided to speak up about it to protect his friends from being bullied by Porky and Corky. Then Mr. Edison with a disappointed look on his face, looked at Porky and Corky who were both sitting at their desks and asked, "Are you two making fun of Bandit and some of the other students in class?" Porky and Corky first looked around the classroom at all the disappointed and angry faces of all the children and with scared and ashamed looks on their faces both answered, "Yes, Mr. Edison, we were making fun of and bullying Bandit and the other students." With a disappointed and puzzled look on his face, Mr. Edison asked Clay to sit back down at his desk, as he thought about how to properly punish the two bullies Porky and Corky and how to help poor Bandit to turn his bad day into a great day. Just then, Mr. Edison looked at the blackboard and saw the fourth activity he planned for the students on their first day of school. The fourth activity Mr. Edison had planned for the children was sure to be one of the children's favorite, a half hour lunch. Mr. Edison thought to himself, "Yes lunchtime would allow me to properly deal with the bullies Corky and Porky, and perhaps help Bandit figure out how to turn his bad day into a great day."

Mr. Edison then looked at the children all sitting at their desks and said, "It is time for lunch." He asked Porky and Corky to stay at their desks and excused the rest of the children as they grabbed their lunches and went outside. Mr. Edison watched as young Bandit slowly left the school and went to the community pond to sit on a bench by himself, still upset about the bad day he was having. Mr. Edison felt bad for poor Bandit and thought to himself, "I will have a talk with poor Bandit as soon as I properly decide how to punish Corky and Porky." Once all the Children were all outside the school eating their lunches, Mr. Edison turned his attention to the bullies Porky and Corky, who were both still sitting at their desks with their heads held down in shame for bullying Bandit and the other children of the Critterville school, and in fear of what Mr. Edison had planned for their punishment. Mr. Edison stood quiet for a few minutes, looking at Porky and Corky thinking of a punishment for them. After thinking about their punishment Mr. Edison said, "Okay Porky and Corky your homework assignment tonight and due tomorrow is first you will write thank you letters to Ranger Woods for the school supplies he gave you and the school. The second homework you will do tonight that is also due tomorrow is you will write a letter to apologize to Bandit and the rest of the children in Critterville school for hurting their feelings and bullying them. The third homework for you tonight is you both go home to your parents as you both will not be allowed to finish the rest of the first day of school. I am sure your parents will have a more proper way of punishing you once I tell them why you have been sent home early from school."

With tears in their eyes, both Corky and Porky said yes to Mr. Edison. With Porky's and Corky's punishment decided, Mr. Edison told Porky and Corky to get their book bags and lunches so he could take the two bullying hedgehog brothers home to their parents. Once outside, Mr. Edison marched Corky and Porky down through Critterville, straight to the Critterville fish market that is owned and operated by Corky's and Porky's parents, Mr. and Mrs. Pine. Mr. and Mrs. Pine who were both busy working at the fish market, both quickly stopped what they were doing, with a concerned look on their faces and watched as their two sons Porky and Corky were being marched into the fish market. Both Porky and Corky had sad but shameful looks on their faces and Mr. Edison had a concerned and disappointed look on his face. Mr and Mrs. Pine rushed over to see what was wrong. With a worried look on her face, Mrs. Pine asked, "What's wrong?" Mr. Edison told Mr. and Mrs. Pine about how Porky and Corky were bullying and making fun of Bandit and the other children at the Critterville school. Mr. Edison went on to tell Mr. and Mrs. Pine about how Corky and Porky had picked on and bullied young Bandit Raccoon. Mr. Edison explained that Corky and Porky took Bandit's lunch and bullied him so much that they had him so upset that tears of sadness ran down his face. Then Mr. Edison told Mr. and Mrs. Pine that finally Corky and Porky tripped Bandit in the classroom as Bandit was passing out the science books and caused several members of the class to get hurt. Mr. Edison went on to say, "I have decided the proper punishment was to send them home for the rest of the day to you. I have given them homework that must be done in order for Corky and Porky to be allowed to return to school."

Mr. and Mrs. Pine looked at their two sons with disappointed looks on their faces as their sons looked back at them with ashamed looks for bullying the children at school and looks of fear as they knew they were in a lot of trouble with their parents. Mr. Pine looked at Mr. Edison and apologized for the way his sons Corky and Porky had behaved in school.

Then Mrs. Pine asked, "Mr. Edison, what are Corky's and Porky's homework assignment?" Mr. Edison responded, "The first homework assignment is for them to write a thank you note to Ranger Woods for giving the Critterville school children school supplies and books for the school. The second one I gave them is to write a letter to apologize to Bandit and the other children at school for making fun of them and bullying them. The third and final assignment I have given them is to write, "I will not bully or make fun of anyone again," 200 times and that is all due tomorrow." Mr. Pine looked at Mr. Edison and replied, "Corky and Porky will have all their homework done before school tomorrow."

Just then Corky and Porky turned to leave the fish market to go home and do their homework. Mr. Pine in an angry voice asked, "Where do you two think you are going?" Corky and Porky both stopped at the sound of their father's angry voice and answered, "Going home to do our homework father." Mr. Pine with a disappointed look on his face replied, "Not yet. First you are going to hear your punishment from your mother and I." Porky and Corky slowly walked back to their mother and father to hear about their punishment from their parents. Mr. Pine looked at his two frightened sons and said, "Your punishment for what you have done in school today is you will both spend the rest of your school day working very hard here at the fish market. Then once the day at the Critterville school is over, you will go home with your mother where she will make sure you do all of your homework your school teacher Mr. Edison has given you." Mr. Pine then said, "You two boys will then go to bed early tonight without desert, but that is not all of your punishment." Mrs. Pine then said, "As part of your punishment for the next week, you boys will do the dishes, and when the fish market closes each night for the next week, you boys will have to come to the fish market and clean and wash the floors." Mrs. Pine with a concerned look on her face as both her and Mr. Pine did not like to punish their sons. Mrs. Pine then said, "We do not want to punish you two boys, but you have to learn and understand that what you boys did to the other children at school was wrong." Mr. Pine looked at Corky and Porky and asked, "Do you boys understand what you did to the other children was wrong?" Then both Porky and Corky with tears in their eyes and feeling ashamed of what they had done to the other children in school answered

Color Me!

Hello to all the kids and grown ups out there! This is Ranger Woods here with my good friend Mr. Edison.

Lets stand together against bullying.

Together we can make a difference.

their father, "Yes, sir." Mr. Edison then thanked Mr. and Mrs. Pine as he shook their hands. Then Mr. Edison turned and looked at Corky and Porky who both had tears running down their faces. Mr. Edison with small tears of his own swelling up in his eyes, put his arms around both boys and said, "Do your homework, come to school tomorrow for a fresh start, and make friends with the other children at school and you see what great friends they can be if you give them a chance. Just then with tears running down all of their faces, Mr. Edison wrapped Porky and Corky in his arms tight and said, "You see you have just made a good friend in me." Mr. Edison said, "You boys do your homework tonight and I will see you in school tomorrow." Once Mr. Edison had everything taken care of with Porky and Corky, he exited the fish market as he wiped the tears from his eyes.

Once outside the fish market, Mr. Edison being the good caring teacher he is, looked around in search of young Bandit. He looked over around the school to see all the children sitting around eating their lunches. Then Mr. Edison looked down at the Critterville community pond and saw young Bandit sitting alone on a bench eating his lunch, as tears of sadness still rolled down his face. Mr. Edison felt real sad for Bandit, knowing how Bandit's first day of school was going. Mr. Edison took his lunch, two sticks with strings and hooks, and went down to the Critterville community pond and sat down on the bench beside Bandit. Mr. Edison looked at Bandit and said, "When I have a bad day I like to go fishing to think." So Mr. Edison handed Bandit a fishing pole and they both sat there fishing in the community pond. Then he told Bandit to cheer up and the rest of the day would go better for him. Bandit replied, "I had a feeling this morning that today was going to be a bad day and so far it is."

With his wisdom, Mr. Edison looked at Bandit and said, "Awe young Bandit if you expect things to go wrong or badly they will, but if you expect good things to happen they will." Then with a smile, Bandit said, "I will think positive thoughts Mr. Edison." Then Bandit with a smile, using the fishing pole Mr. Edison had given him caught a big catfish. Bandit with a big smile on his face yelled, "Look at the big catfish I caught Mr. Edison!" With a big smile and tears of happiness Mr. Edison replied, "You see Bandit if you think positive thoughts good things will happen." With a big smile on his little face, Bandit hugged Mr. Edison and said, "Thank you Mr. Edison." Mr. Edison replied, "You are very welcome Bandit." Bandit asked, "Mr. Edison, may I run home and show my dad my big catfish?" "It's your lunchtime until I ring the school bell," replied Mr. Edison.

Bandit gave his teacher another big hug and thanked him again before running to his home to show his dad his catfish. Then with tears of happiness swelling up in his eyes and a big smile on his face Mr. Edison thought to himself that maybe thinking positive thoughts would work for him too. Just then Mr. Edison caught a big fish on his fishing pole. With a big smile Mr. Edison said, "It does work," as he put the fish back into the community pond and headed back to the school.

Meanwhile with his big catfish, in his hand Bandit ran as fast as he could through Critterville, all the way to his home and his mother's and father's business. Once Bandit arrived at his home he found his mother and father, both standing outside in front of their home. After running as fast as he could from the community pond to his home, Bandit took a few seconds to catch his breath, and he began telling his parents about the bad day he was having on the first day of school. Then he told his parents, that during lunch, he was sitting at community pond by himself feeling bad about how the first day of school was going, when Mr. Edison sat down beside him on the bench, and gave him a fishing pole. Bandit explained to his parents that Mr. Edison told him to think positive, and good thoughts, I caught this big catfish. "Mr. Edison was right Papa, I thought positive and good things started happening."

Then Bandit's father Mr. Raccoon took the big catfish from Bandit and with a big smile said, "I am proud of you Bandit." Mrs. Raccoon with a happy smile said, "To celebrate your first day of school, we will have your catfish for dinner." Bandit looked at his mother with a big smile and said, "Thanks mom." Just then Bandit heard Mr. Edison ringing the school bell to let the children know lunch time was over, and it was time to come back into the school. Bandit hugged his parents, and ran back to school thinking positive thoughts. Mr. and Mrs. Raccoon were both very happy, and proud of their son, as they watched him run back and disappear into the school. Then Mr. Raccoon looked at Mrs. Raccoon and could see she was still a little worried about Bandit. With a smile on his face, Mr. Raccoon hugged Mrs. Raccoon and said, "Bandit will be fine with Mr. Edison to teach him." Mrs. Raccoon looked at Mr. Raccoon with a smile and replied, "You are right dear," and gave Mr. Raccoon a hug, as they both went back to work in their furniture and tailor shops.

Meanwhile, back at the Critterville school, the school was getting better for Bandit, as he only had positive thoughts. Bandit passed the spelling test getting all ten spelling words right. He also passed his math test, and his science test only getting one question wrong. Mr. Edison was very happy for Bandit the way things were going for him. Then Mr.

Edison gave the children their homework assignments, at the end of the first day of school in Critterville and dismissed the children to go home. All the children grabbed their books and left except Bandit. With a smile on his face; Bandit went up to Mr. Edison and placed an apple on his desk and said, "Thank you teacher." With tears swelling in his eyes and a smile Mr. Edison said, "You are very welcome Bandit."

With his books in his hands and a smile on his face, Bandit ran home to complete his homework, and to help his father in the furniture shop. Both Bandit and Bonnie finished their homework in a few minutes. Then the both of them changed their school clothes into their old clothes and went to help their parents. Bonnie went to the kitchen to help her mother to prepare the Raccoon family dinner with Bandit's big catfish, as the main dish. Bandit went to help his father Mr. Raccoon finish making a table for the stork Mr. Flag the Critterville mailman, and paint the chairs for the swan Mrs. Snow's boarding house.

Bandit and Mr. Raccoon had just finished painting Mrs. Snow's chairs, and Mr. Flag's table, when the door opened up in the shop and in came Mr. Pine and his two sons Porky and Corky. Just as Mr. Raccoon was asking Mr. Pine how may I help you, the door opened up again and it was Mr. Edison. Mr. Raccoon said, "Hello how can I help you folks?"

Mr. Pine replied, "Well Mr. Raccoon first my two sons are here to apologize to young Bandit for being mean, and bullying him today in school." Then Mr. Pine in a serious tone of voice, asked his two sons, "Do you have something to say to Bandit?" Both Porky and Corky with sad and ashamed looks on their faces, looked at Bandit and said, "We are sorry for the way we treated you today in school." They asked if they could be friends. With a happy face he walked over to them, and said, "It's alright guys. I would be happy to have you both for friends." Then they all shook hands.

With a smile on his face and tears of happiness swelling in his eyes Mr. Raccoon looked at Mr. Pine and asked, "Is there anything else I can help you with Mr. Pine?" With a smile on his face, Mr. Pine replied, "Yes Mr. Raccoon, I would like to place an order for a new table and four chairs." Mr. Raccoon said, "I can do that for you," as he shook Mr. Pine's hand. Mr. Pine said, "Thank you and good night," as he and his two sons left the furniture shop. Then Mr. Raccoon asked, "How can I help you Mr. Edison?" Mr. Edison answered, "I'd like to place a furniture order for a desk and a chair to put in my home." Mr. Raccoon wrote the order and told Mr. Edison he would have it ready for him next week. "That would be great!" replied Mr. Edison.

Then Mr. Edison looked over at Bandit and said, "I have something for you Bandit." Mr. Edison then handed Bandit a book bag with all the school supplies inside. Bandit had a big smile on his face, as he thanked Mr. Edison. Mr. Edison replied, "You are very welcome Bandit and remember think positive thoughts." Still with a smile on his face, Bandit replied, "Yes sir! Mr. Edison." Mr. Raccoon shook Mr. Edison's hand and said, "Thank you." Just then the door opened up again in the furniture shop. Bonnie entered and said, hello to Mr. Edison, and told Mr. Raccoon and Bandit that dinner was done. Mr Raccoon answered, "Okay Bonnie we will be right there, as soon as we lock up." Bonnie said, "Okay Papa," and went back to the house.

Mr. Raccoon, Bandit, and Mr. Edison all left the furniture shop as Mr. Raccoon locked the door. Once outside Mr. Edison asked, "What are you having for dinner that smells so good?" Bandit answered, "My mother cooked the big catfish I caught at the community pond." With a big smile on his face Mr. Raccoon asked, "Mr. Edison would you like to have dinner with us?" With an excited voice Bandit said, "Please eat dinner with us, Mr. Edison." With a smile on his face, Mr. Edison replied, "I would be honored to eat dinner with you folks." Mr. Raccoon, Bandit, and Mr. Edison all went into the raccoon home, and washed up for dinner. Mrs. Raccoon made a tasty dinner that included the catfish, mashed potatoes, peas, iced tea to drink and for dessert was a yummy blueberry pie. Mr. Edison and the Raccoon family enjoyed each other's company so much that Mr. Edison stayed there talking, laughing, and drinking iced tea until dark.

Then Mr. Edison thanked the Raccoon family for the tasty dinner, as he got up to leave and asked Bonnie and Bandit if they would like to help him to deliver the Critterville newspapers in the morning. Bandit and Bonnie both answered, "Yes Sir!" Then Mrs. Raccoon told Bandit and Bonnie to get ready for bed. Bandit and Bonnie hugged their parents and Mr. Edison as they said, good night as they went to bed. Then Mrs. Raccoon said, good night to Mr. Edison as she went off to bed. Mr. Raccoon went outside with Mr. Edison and said, "Thank you for helping

Bandit at school today, as well as for the other children." "The children here in Critterville are good and very important to me, that's why I became a teacher. You are very welcome Mr. Raccoon and shook hands and said good night to each other," replied Mr. Edison.

Before going to bed Mr. and Mrs. Raccoon went in to check on their children. They checked on Bonnie first, but she was fast asleep. Mr. Raccoon pulled up the blanket over her. They both kissed her on the forehead. Then went over to check on Bandit. Bandit was still awake. They told him they were proud of him for being so brave on his first day of school. As they both kissed him on the forehead and said good night. As they were leaving Bandit said, "I can't wait till tomorrow." Mrs. Raccoon laughed and said, "The faster you go to sleep the sooner the tomorrow will be here." Then she said, "Good night son," as she was heading to her room. Bandit fell asleep with a big smile on his face, as he dreamed of the second day of school in Critterville.

LESSON:

Maybe we humans, children and grown ups alike can learn a few lessons from the critters in the Adventures of Critterville.

As children who are friends of someone being bullied, we should stand with our friends against the bullies, not with a fist but together going to the teachers or parents, and telling them about the bullying and who is doing the bullying. We as teachers and parents, with a clear mind need to help the children being bullied and confront the bullies not in anger, but with a stern voice to make the child doing the bullying seeing the pain that such actions can cause someone else. I believe nine times out of ten, most bullies are good kids and once an adult steps in, a bully and the child being bullied become great friends. In my experience all to often teachers, as well as parents just ignore bullying, and need to address every bullying situation and complaint no matter how big or small. I believe we ignore it as much as I believe we become so busy in our own lives, we don't notice the bullying going around us. We as grownups can help prevent, and stop bullying and save all the children involved in this serious painful situation. As for the children doing the bullying try going to the children you have bullied and try being nice and get to really know them, as I believe you will find a great friend in them. Try saying you are sorry, shake their hands, and make a new great friend. Stand with your friends against bullies.

Hello Jr. Rangers:
We have included two picture posters for you to cut out and hang in your room or in you school locker. Remember to treat others the way you want to be treated. Be kind and don't bully or make fun of others. We hope you enjoyed this story.